W9-BLG-561

E SPU
Spurr, Elizabeth.
The Peterkins' Thanksgiving
/ Elizabeth Spurr ;
illustrated by Wendy
Halperin.

FOUNTAINDALE PUBLIC LIBRARY DISTRICT
300 West Briarcliff Road
Bolingbrook, IL 60440-2894
(630) 759-2102

the Peterkins' Thanksgiving

Adapted by Elizabeth Spurr

from the original story by

Lucretia P. Hale

Illustrated by Wendy Anderson Halperin

ATHENEUM BOOKS FOR YOUNG READERS New York London Toronto Sydney

Dear Lady from Philadelphia,

  We are sorry you had to return home so suddenly. The family
had looked forward to sharing Thanksgiving dinner with you.
But, as things turned out, perhaps it was just as well . . .

The air was crisp; the leaves had turned;

the harvest had been gathered. Now, the Peterkins busied themselves
preparing a grand dinner to celebrate a day of thanks as their Pilgrim
ancestors had done more than two centuries before.

 Mrs. Peterkin had laid the dining-room table with her best linen
cloth and silver candlesticks. Elizabeth Eliza fashioned a horn-of-
plenty centerpiece from gourds and dried corn. The Little Boys
gathered autumn leaves to surround the centerpiece. And Agamemnon
spent the afternoon reading a book, in order to provide some intelligent
dinner conversation.

Dressed in their Sunday clothes, the eight Peterkins circled their dining table, as savory aromas of the feast wafted from the kitchen below.

After the blessing, the family sat. Mrs. Peterkin tinkled her small china bell, used only on special occasions, signaling Amanda, the cook, to send the feast upstairs.

Nothing happened.

 . . . *for the meal was substantially delayed, due to an odd circumstance.*

"You know very well, my dear," Mr. Peterkin said with a grunt, "Amanda can't hear that bell."

"No matter," said Mrs. Peterkin. "She'll dish up when she hears our chairs scraping the floor above her."

"Then where is the dinner?" Mr. Peterkin rose and clanged on an old ship's watch bell, which hung near the fireplace. Mrs. Peterkin had thought the bell quite useless since their home was a great distance from the sea.

A moment later Amanda scurried into the room. "The dinner, sir, it's stuck!"

"In the oven?" said Mrs. Peterkin. "I knew that turkey was too large."

"In the kettles?" said Elizabeth Eliza. "Did you burn the vegetables?"

"In the dumbwaiter!" cried Amanda. "It won't budge!"

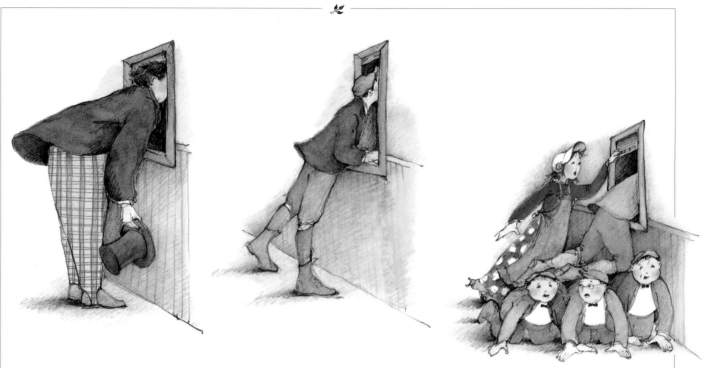

Mr. Peterkin, Agamemnon, and Solomon John took turns looking down the opening of the dumbwaiter, where a platform attached to cords would lift their dinner to the dining room from the kitchen below. They yanked on the cords. There was the rattle of china, but no dinner appeared.

"I'm hungry," said Solomon John.

"There's only one course of action," said Agamemnon, who, because he had been to college, was relied upon for answers. "We must eat downstairs in the kitchen."

"I'm not too proud to eat in the kitchen," said Mr. Peterkin. With napkin in hand he moved to the staircase, followed by Elizabeth Eliza and her gourds and dried corn. The Little Boys brought their crisp autumn leaves, which were in fairly small bits because before gathering them, they couldn't resist stomping through them with their india-rubber boots.

After setting the kitchen table, Amanda went to the dumbwaiter. She returned, wringing her hands. "Sorry, sir. The dinner's stuck halfway up."

Mr. Peterkin looked toward the ceiling. "What exactly *was* our dinner?"

"With the turkey, there was oyster dressing," said Mrs. Peterkin.

"Squash and tomatoes," said Amanda.

"White and sweet potatoes," said Elizabeth Eliza.

"Umm, sweet potatoes," said the Little Boys.

Mrs. Peterkin tried to find a bright spot. "Thank goodness I didn't make cranberry sauce."

"I don't like oyster dressing, anyway," said Solomon John, anxious to help.

Elizabeth Eliza added, "And I don't much fancy squash."

"If that's the way you feel," Mrs. Peterkin said, sighing, "perhaps we'd better leave the dinner where it is."

"After a few days," said Agamemnon, "I'm afraid the odor would grow unpleasant."

"Besides, I'm hungry," said Solomon John.

"Why don't we eat the pumpkin pies?" said the Little Boys. They pointed to the pastries, still cooling on the counter.

"You know the rule," said Mr. Peterkin firmly. "No dessert until you've eaten all your victuals."

 *If only you had been here to advise us, things might have gone better.*

"I have an idea," said Agamemnon, who had just peered up through the dumbwaiter opening. "The dinner seems to be just below the kitchen ceiling. If I had a ladder and an axe, I could cut through the wall and reach it."

"Wouldn't it be better to call the carpenter?" asked Elizabeth Eliza.

"Perhaps it would," said Mrs. Peterkin. "Especially since we have no ladder and no axe."

So Mr. Peterkin, Solomon John, and the Little Boys went to find the carpenter, the same reliable man who had rebuilt the parlor ceiling when the Christmas tree was too tall.

Meanwhile, Agamemnon went, as usual, to find the solution in a book. "This affair of the turkey," he said, "reminds me of those buried cities that have been dug out—Herculaneum, for instance. They uncovered many kitchen pots, even some preserved pies and hams. I think they did that with a pickaxe."

Obtaining help was not a simple matter, . . .

Mr. Peterkin hitched the horse to the carryall. Solomon John hopped in, followed by the Little Boys. He took the reins, and the horse started off merrily but then suddenly stopped and would go no farther.

Solomon John shook the reins and pulled them and clucked to the horse. Mr. Peterkin shouted, and the Little Boys whistled and whinnied, but the horse would not go.

"We will have to whip him," said Mr. Peterkin.

"I do not like to whip animals," said Solomon John. "Perhaps we can give him a tug."

So he and the Little Boys jumped from the rig and tugged with all their might. They tugged so hard they pulled the ring from the hitching post, for Mr. Peterkin had forgotten to untie the horse!

Off went the cart, with Solomon John and the Little Boys panting to catch up.

"Sorry," said Mr. Peterkin, when his passengers finally overtook him. "I was afraid to stop lest the horse not start again."

 . . . *for the carpenter was out of town.*

At the carpenter's house Mr. Peterkin was told that the man was dining out of town with relatives. "But he will return tonight," said his housekeeper, "in time to ring the nine o'clock bell at the church."

"I guess our dinner will have to wait," said Mr. Peterkin, putting on a cheerful face.

At home the family passed the time listening to Agamemnon read about Herculaneum, until, irritable with hunger, they begged Mrs. Peterkin to put on tea.

"How can we have tea, my dears," she said, "when we have not yet had dinner?"

"That would hardly be proper," said Elizabeth Eliza.

"We're hungry," said Solomon John and the Little Boys.

What would you, dear lady, have done?

Mrs. Peterkin wondered, "What would the wise lady from Philadelphia advise in a case like this?"

Mr. Peterkin patted his belly. "I think she would say, 'Let them who want tea have it; the rest can go without.'"

So the whole family sat down to tea, but little was eaten because all agreed, upon consideration, that they should not spoil their appetites.

When the nine o'clock bell was heard, Agamemnon, Solomon John, and the Little Boys rushed to the church and found the carpenter.

"Bring your ladder and axe," they called to him.

"And a pickaxe!" Agamemnon shouted.

The carpenter, thinking the house must be on fire, brought his water buckets, too.

When he arrived at the Peterkins', the family, all talking at once, tried to explain the problem. The carpenter went into the dining room, untwisted a cord, arranged the weight, and pulled up the dinner.

"The trouble was the weight," said the carpenter.

"I should say so," said Mrs. Peterkin. "I've never waited so long for any meal."

"Patient waiters are no losers," Agamemnon said.

ᕙ *At long last dinner was served, and we all acknowledged it was worth the wait.*

Amanda warmed up the vegetables, pulled the cords, and sent the covered dishes steaming to the table. Elizabeth Eliza raced downstairs to retrieve her gourds and dried corn, but the Little Boys, in their haste to claim the turkey drumsticks, forgot the autumn leaves.

"Dumb waiter," one said, giggling between bites.

"No," said the other, "*dumb* dumbwaiter."

"That only goes to prove," said Agamemnon, "the value

of an education."

🌿 *We hope you had a pleasant holiday. Please* do *try to join*
us for our Christmas meal.
Sincerely yours,
Elizabeth Eliza Peterkin

For the six Spurrs; I am thankful.
—E. S.

Thank you, Mom and Dad, for so many turkeys,
trimmings, and things to be thankful for.
—W. A. H.

Atheneum Books for Young Readers
An imprint of Simon & Schuster Children's Publishing Division
1230 Avenue of the Americas
New York, New York 10020

Text copyright © 2005 by Elizabeth Spurr
Illustrations copyright © 2005 by Wendy Anderson Halperin
All rights reserved, including the right of reproduction in whole or in part in any form.

Book design by Sonia Chaghatzbanian
The text of this book is set in Caslon.
The illustrations of this book are rendered in watercolors.

Manufactured in China
First Edition

2 4 6 8 10 9 7 5 3 1

Library of Congress Cataloging-in-Publication Data
Spurr, Elizabeth.
The Peterkins' Thanksgiving / Elizabeth Spurr ; illustrated by Wendy Anderson Halperin.—1st ed.
p.   cm.
Summary: As the eccentric Peterkin family sits down to Thanksgiving dinner, they learn that their
turkey and the rest of the food has become stuck in the dumbwaiter.
ISBN 0-689-84142-6 (ISBN-13: 978-0-689-84142-2)
[1. Thanksgiving Day—Fiction. 2. Family life—Fiction. 3. Humorous stories.]
I. Halperin, Wendy Anderson, ill. II. Title.
PZ7.S7695Pg 2005
[Fic]—dc21   2003004960